TOTALLY
ROAR-SOME
DINOSAUR
ACTIVITIES

First published 2017 by Parragon Books, Ltd.

Copyright © 2019 Cottage Door Press, LLC
5005 Newport Drive
Rolling Meadows, Illinois 60008

Written by Mandy Archer
Illustrated by Gareth Lucas

ISBN: 978-1-68052-683-7

Parragon Books is an imprint of Cottage Door Press, LLC.
Parragon Books® and the Parragon® logo
are registered trademarks of Cottage Door Press, LLC.

TOTALLY ROAR-SOME DINOSAUR ACTIVITIES

PaRragon®

Who's hatching?

Peeping dino,
keep your cool.
What is lurking
in the pool?

Turn this tiny twosome into a huge, happy herd.

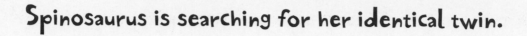

Spinosaurus is searching for her identical twin.

Use greens and blues to bring her spiny sister to life.

Gaze at the rows of scaly toes ...
doodle the dinosaurs they belong to!

An enormous dinosaur
lurks in this cave! Use your
imagination to bring him into the light.

Ro ar!

Draw who, or what, is making that noise.

Color the scales of this
SCARY T. rex!

Color in the shadows to complete this dinosaur pattern.

START

Baby triceratops
needs to find his way
to the watering hole!

Put crocs
on the
rocks!

How many frogs can you find?

Use your sketching skills to put the dinosaurs back in the picture!

Add . . .

4 x

3 x

2 x

1 x

What a lot of dino babies!

Make every tiny triceratops look different from its brothers and sisters.

Mama dinosaur's babies look just like her!
Sketch seven teeny T. rex
snapping their tiny teeth.

Draw some eye-popping dinosaur tails.

Will they be spiky, silly, or slithery?

What is lurking in the water? Connect the dots, then color in the creatures of the deep.

What's for dinner, diplodocus?

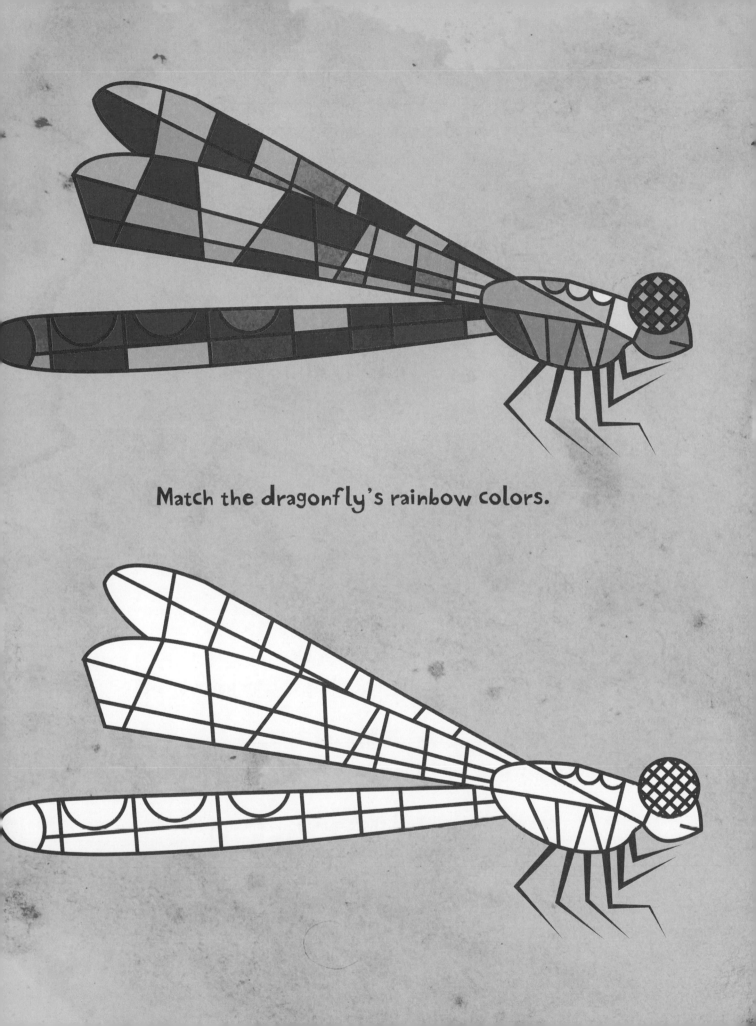

Match the dragonfly's rainbow colors.

Find a friend, then play a game of swamp squares!

HOW TO PLAY
Take turns connecting two dots on the game board.

Every time you draw a line that completes a square,
write your initial inside, then take another turn.

Keep going until all the squares are completed.
The player with the most points is the winner.

Empty square = 1 POINT   = 2 POINTS   = 5 POINTS

Camouflage these little dinosaurs in the jungle!

Doodle dinosaurs
meeting at the
water's edge!

Which two green dinos are exactly the same?

Tickly tentacles! Draw more ammonites swimming in their shells.

Thud!

Thud!

Thud!

Thud!

Who are these tiny, timid dinosaurs running away from?

Who's chasing who?
Add some more
dizzy dinosaurs!

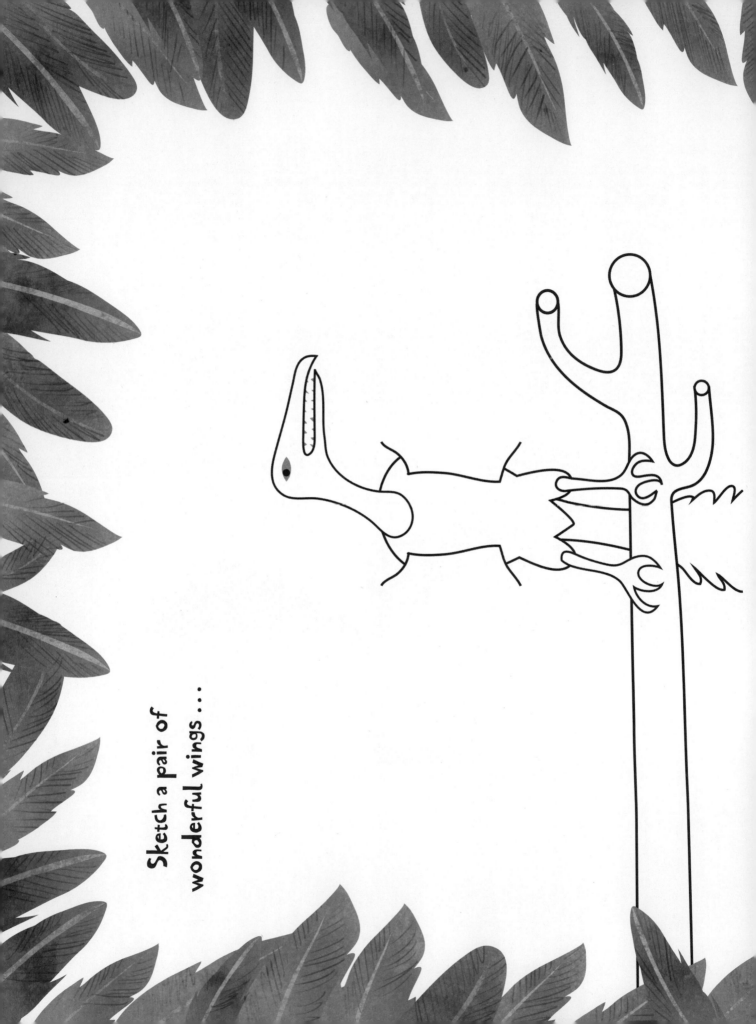

Sketch a pair of wonderful wings . . .

...then add a stunning plume of tail feathers!

Six sneaky dinosaurs are hiding in the forest. Find the first one, then draw five more.

Never wake a sleeping dinosaur!

Fill his head with dinosaur dreams instead.

Answers: 10 have yellow eyes; 12 have stripy bodies; 7 have green wings.

Add fearsome faces, flashing eyes, and terrible teeth.

A creature from the deep

A tough triceratops

A cracking dinosaur egg

Have your pencils ready!

A swooping pterosaur

A dramatic dragonfly

A massive giganotosaurus!

Dotty shapes, lurking lumps,
draw the dino's humps and bumps!

Fill the sky with flying friends.

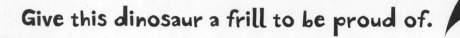
Give this dinosaur a frill to be proud of.

You've met the dinosaur babies...now draw Mom and Dad!

Phew! It gets hot in the desert.

Draw the details to finish these twins.

Now sketch
some more
fierce friends,
scuttling around
the page.

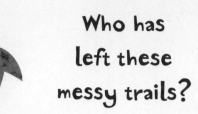

Who has
left these
messy trails?

How many dinosaurs
are in the herd?

Turn over for
the answer!

When you've finished with the other side of this page, make a triceratops mask!

(There were 31 dinosaurs in the herd!)

Color in the face, then ask a grown-up to help you cut it out and stick it onto some white cardboard, and to cut along all the dotted lines.

Press a pen through the black dots on each side of the mask to make a hole on each side. Tie a piece of elastic through each hole. Use this to attach the mask to your head.

Ready? It's time to dinosaur ROAR

What a lot of dotty dinosaurs!
Trace the dots, add
patterns and color.

It's easy to get lost in the swamp.
Help the dinosaur find his friend.

START

FINISH

Who is chasing the little yellow dinosaur?

START

This brave dino is following a trail. Use the key to help him get all the way to the end.

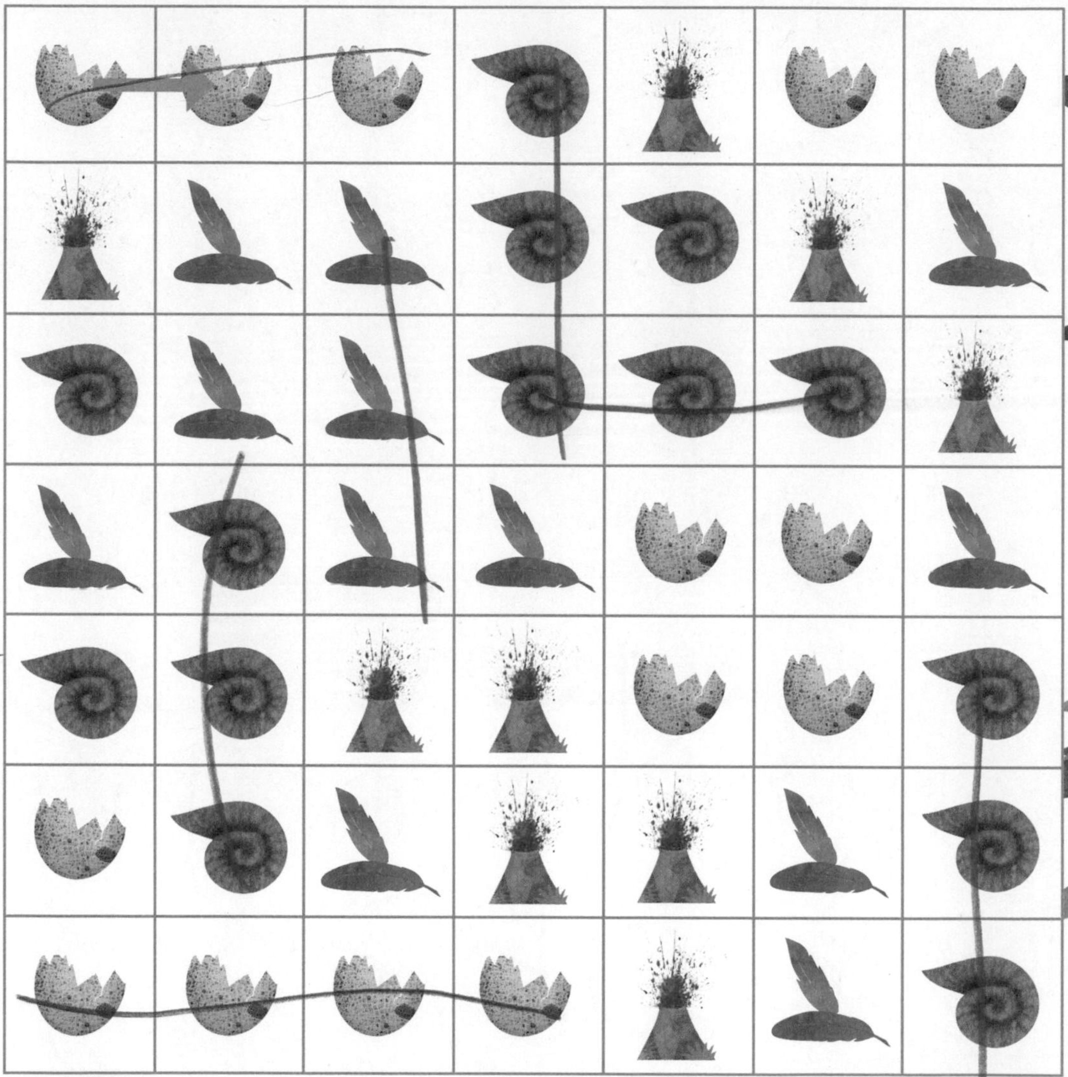

KEY

FINISH

= ONE STEP LEFT

= ONE STEP UP

= ONE STEP DOWN

= ONE STEP RIGHT

Create a cool comic strip story. Ready, steady, doodle!

THERE ONCE WAS A VERY SHY DINOSAUR ...

ROOARRRRR!

THE DINOSAUR RUSHED OUT OF HIS CAVE ...

THE END

T. rex has **terrible** claws and **terrible** jaws!

Sketch him a set of teeth to **flash** and **snap**.

Draw some more bones for T. rex to **gnash** and **gnaw!**

Stare at this page for **60** seconds.
Try to remember everything you see.

Now turn over . . .

Try to remember . . .

1 ③
How many purple dinosaurs were there?

2 purple
What color was the slithery snake?

3
How many ancient dragonflies did you see?

4
What color were the pterosaur's wings?

5
How many horns did the triceratops have?

6
What pattern was on the orange dinosaur's body?

When you've finished, color in this smart stegosaurus!

Who's lurking in the deep, dark jungle?

These pterosaurs are missing their wings! Color them in.

Psstt! This T. rex wants to tell you a story ...
Use your imagination to write his amazing tale.

....

....

....

....

....

....

....

....

What creatures are lurking on this page? Read the clues, then draw a pair of dinosaurs that match the description.

I HAVE A BIG BODY.

1. There are spines on the end of my tail.

2. Armored plates run all along my back.

3. I stand on four legs.

I AM TALL AND TOUGH.

1. I have tiny arms.

2. I stand on two legs.

3. My teeth are supersharp.

BEWARE!

This volcano is going to blow!
Color in a path to solid ground.

START

FINISH

What a squish and a squeeze!

Let the dinosaur battle begin!

VERSUS

This **daring dinosaur** is hoping for a fish supper!

Can you spot five **differences** between these two pictures?

Eek! Diplodocus alert!
Doodle some tiny
dinosaurs darting
out of the way.

Use your doodling
skills to bring the
dinosaur herd to life.

Trudge! Stomp! Stamp!

Look at each row, then draw the next dinosaur in the sequence for each one.

Clawsome!

Cover this dinosaur in colorful patterns.

The forest is very quiet.

Who can you see in the trees?

Watch out!

This pterosaur is swooping
down from the sky!

Add some flying friends!

Design a dinosaur! Sketch a brand-new species.

....

Write your dinosaur's name here.